STAR WARS®

THE CHEWBACCA STORY

Adapted by Benjamin Harper

studio fun

A READER'S DIGEST COMPANY

White Plains, New York • Montréal, Québec • Bath, United Kingdom

Chewbacca is one of the greatest heroes in the *Star Wars* galaxy. He is a Wookiee from a beautiful planet named Kashyyyk. Wookiees live in the forests on Kashyyyk and speak a language called Shyriiwook that sounds like growls, roars, and barks.

Although best known for his heroic role in conflicts against the Empire and the First Order, Chewbacca fought many battles on the side of good long before the Empire took control of the galaxy.

During the Clone Wars, he helped free Jedi younglings. He also fought valiantly in the Battle of Kachirho on his home planet when droid armies invaded, and helped Jedi Master Yoda escape a sinister plot to wipe out the Jedi.

Along the way, the loyal Wookiee befriended Han Solo, pilot of the *Millennium Falcon*, and struck up a partnership that led to many adventures together.

Chewbacca became first mate and copilot of the *Millennium Falcon*. He was in a cantina in Mos Eisley spaceport on Tatooine when an old man approached him about a job. Jedi Master Obi-Wan Kenobi and his apprentice, Luke Skywalker, needed a way off Tatooine. R2-D2, a droid traveling with them, was carrying secret plans to the Death Star—the Empire's secret weapon— and had to get to Alderaan.

Chewie introduced Obi-Wan to Han.  Han agreed to take them all to Alderaan. They needed to leave right away.

As Han made final preparations, stormtroopers arrived and started firing. "Chewie, get us out of here!" Han yelled as he got on the ship. Chewie howled. The *Falcon* blasted away from Tatooine!

Star Destroyers chased them, but Han and Chewie piloted the ship into hyperspace!

When they arrived at where they expected to find Alderaan, they discovered that the planet was gone. The Death Star had destroyed it! As they flew through chunks of space rock, Chewie roared. The *Falcon* headed uncontrollably toward the Death Star, caught in a tractor beam that dragged them onto the space station. They had to hide. Han had secret compartments in his ship. They climbed into them and waited.

Stormtroopers searched the ship, and Han and Luke took possession of some stormtrooper armor. Then the *Falcon* crew went to a command center. Obi-Wan left to turn off the tractor beam. R2-D2 discovered that Princess Leia, who had given R2 the secret plans to protect, was a prisoner on the Death Star. They had to save her!

Luke had an idea. He found some binders to make Chewbacca look like a prisoner. Chewie roared!  Luke gave the binders to Han, who put them on Chewbacca. They left R2 and C-3PO, a protocol droid, behind and went to the detention area where Princess Leia was being held.

Chewbacca broke free!  He helped Han and Luke fight the guards. They freed the princess but they were trapped. Then Leia blasted a hole in a grate. They jumped through the hole into a garbage chute. Chewbacca howled. As the walls started to close in on them, Luke contacted C-3PO and had R2 turn off the trash compactor. Now they needed to get back to the *Millennium Falcon*!

Chewbacca and Han Solo fought stormtroopers through the halls. They made it back to the hangar. In the meantime, Obi-Wan deactivated the tractor beam, but then he sacrificed himself in a fight with Darth Vader, a Sith Lord in service to the Emperor, so his friends could escape.

Chewie and Han blasted the *Falcon* away from the Death Star.

Now TIE fighters attacked them! As Chewbacca piloted the *Falcon*, Han and Luke battled the fighters. Then they flew toward the rebel base on Yavin 4. But the Death Star tracked them. The Empire planned to destroy the rebel base!

Han wanted to leave. Chewbacca knew staying and helping the rebels was the right thing to do, but he went with Han.

The rebels attacked the Death Star. Luke piloted an X-wing. He had just one chance to destroy the Death Star before it fired on the rebel base! Darth Vader followed in a TIE fighter, when a blast that came out of nowhere fired on his ship. Han and Chewie had returned!

With Darth Vader spinning away from the battle, Luke fired—and hit the target! The Death Star exploded and the rebels were safe!

In a ceremony on Yavin 4, Princess Leia awarded Luke and Han medals. Chewbacca stood at their side as the rebels cheered. Chewbacca roared!

Three years later, Chewie and Han were on Hoth, an icy planet where the rebels had their new base. Making repairs on the *Millennium Falcon*, Chewbacca growled as he worked.

When the rebels picked up a strange code on their scanners, Chewbacca and Han went out to investigate. Chewbacca howled when he spotted an Imperial probe droid. It fired at Chewie, and Han blew it up. The Empire now knew the location of the rebel base. Everyone had to leave!

Chewbacca readied the *Millennium Falcon* for takeoff. Han, Leia, and C-3PO raced through the tunnels. Chewbacca was waiting for them at the ship.  They boarded just as Imperial troops invaded the base!

But there was trouble—the *Falcon* wasn't working! Chewie growled. "Come on!" Han yelled to Chewie, who ran into the cockpit. Finally, the ship started and they blasted away from Hoth. Then, when Han tried to jump to hyperspace, the ship didn't move. Now they were pursued by Star Destroyers!

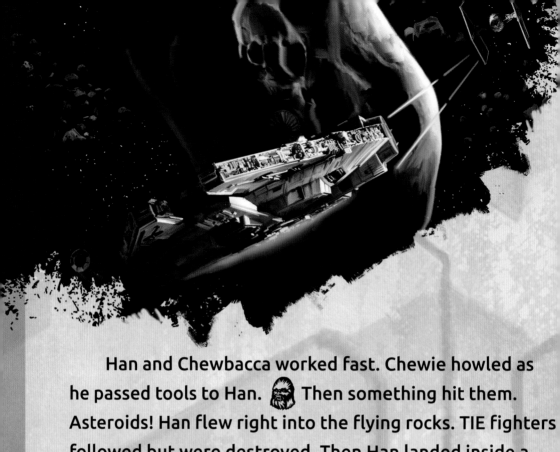

Han and Chewbacca worked fast. Chewie howled as he passed tools to Han.  Then something hit them. Asteroids! Han flew right into the flying rocks. TIE fighters followed but were destroyed. Then Han landed inside a giant asteroid so they could work on the ship.

But Chewie and Han couldn't fix the hyperdrive on the *Falcon.* So Han piloted to Cloud City where his friend Lando Calrissian lived. Lando could help them. "How are you doing, Chewbacca?" Lando said when they met. Chewie roared hello. Lando promised to help them. But the Empire had followed them and was setting a trap.

Then C-3PO went missing. Chewbacca found C-3PO's parts in a junk pile. Ugnaughts were going to melt him down! Chewbacca howled  as he grabbed C-3PO's parts. He rescued the droid!

After that, Lando took them all to Darth Vader. Chewbacca roared when he saw the sinister Dark Lord. Darth Vader took Han prisoner and placed Chewbacca's friend in a carbon freeze unit. Chewbacca howled as his friend was frozen and given to Boba Fett, a bounty hunter who had followed them to Cloud City. Boba Fett would take Han to Jabba the Hutt, a crime lord to whom Han owed money.

Chewbacca and Leia were now Darth Vader's prisoners. Lando knew he had to help them. "We're getting out of here," he said, as he freed Chewbacca and Leia from stormtroopers. Chewbacca roared as they raced to the platform where Boba Fett's ship was located. But they were too late! Boba Fett blasted off into space.

Then they ran into R2-D2, who had come to
Cloud City with Luke Skywalker. They all rushed to
the *Millennium Falcon* and blasted away! But as they
flew, Leia sensed that Luke was in trouble. She asked
Chewbacca to turn the ship around. He roared in
agreement.

They found Luke on an antenna beneath
Cloud City. He had been fighting Darth Vader.
Chewbacca piloted the ship underneath Luke, while
Lando rescued him. Now they needed to leave! But
the hyperdrive was still broken. Chewbacca growled
as he tried to fix it.

At last, R2-D2 managed to repair it. They soared
into hyperspace and joined the rebel fleet.

Lando and Chewbacca had to rescue Han Solo. Chewbacca growled goodbye  to his friends Luke and Leia, who stayed behind. Then he flew the *Millennium Falcon* toward Tatooine.

Chewbacca, Luke, Leia, Lando, and the droids fought Jabba and his minions to save Han Solo. Once they rescued him, they all flew away from Tatooine. Chewbacca was glad to see his friend again!

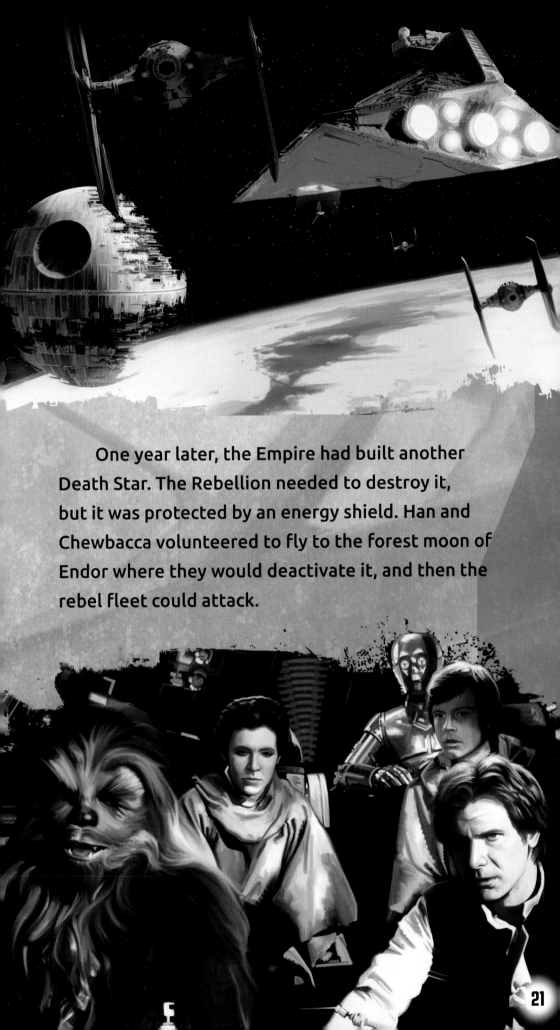

One year later, the Empire had built another Death Star. The Rebellion needed to destroy it, but it was protected by an energy shield. Han and Chewbacca volunteered to fly to the forest moon of Endor where they would deactivate it, and then the rebel fleet could attack.

On Endor, Chewbacca smelled food. He howled and ran to get it. ![Chewbacca] But it was a trap! They were captured by the Ewoks. At the Ewoks' village, C-3PO talked the Ewoks into helping the rebels. The Ewoks showed Han and Chewbacca where the Empire's shield generator was.

The rebels broke into the Empire's base—but they were captured! Han, Chewbacca, Leia, and the droids surrendered. Then the Ewoks attacked, and a great battle took place. Chewbacca howled ![Chewbacca] as he swung with two Ewoks to an Imperial walker. He took over the walker and walked it to the Imperial bunker.

The rebels and Ewoks won the ground battle! They blew up the shield and the rebel fleet attacked the Death Star.

After the Death Star exploded, the Ewoks and rebels had a great celebration. Chewbacca and his friends danced. The galaxy was free!

Many years later, Han and Chewie were piloting a giant freighter when they discovered the *Millennium Falcon* in space above the planet Jakku. They captured the ship and boarded it. "Chewie, we're home!" Han said. Chewie roared.

They found Rey, a scavenger; Finn, a former stormtrooper; and BB-8, an astromech droid, on board. BB-8 needed to get to the Resistance base. He had a map to find Luke Skywalker, who was missing!

But something else was happening on Han's ship!
Chewie and Han raced to see what it was. The Guavian
Death Gang and Kanjiklub were on board! Han owed
both gangs money. They were here to collect!

Rey snuck over to a control panel. She hit a button
and released dangerous rathtars that Han and Chewie
were transporting.

Chewie roared 🐾 as he and Han ran through the
halls away from the rathtars and both gangs.

Chewie and Han made their way to the docking bay where the *Falcon* was. Chewie got hurt!  He howled, but managed to get onto the *Falcon*. Finn helped Chewbacca as Rey and Han piloted the *Falcon* away from the freighter.

They went to Takodana to meet Maz Kanata, Han's old friend. While they were there, the First Order showed up. The First Order wanted BB-8 and the map so they could find Luke Skywalker first!

As he fought off First Order stormtroopers, Chewbacca roared.  The rough battle ended when Kylo Ren of the First Order took Rey prisoner. She had seen the map, so Kylo thought they no longer needed BB-8, since he could read her mind. Kylo took Rey away on a ship.

Back on the Resistance base, they came up with a plan. The First Order had a giant weapon called Starkiller Base, and had destroyed the New Republic. The Resistance was next, so they had to act fast.

Chewbacca, Han, and Finn would fly to the base and deactivate the shield. Then the Resistance could fly in and disable the weapon!

Han, Chewbacca, and Finn soared through hyperspace. Chewie roared  as they came in for a crash landing on Starkiller Base, the *Millennium Falcon* bursting through trees and skidding to a stop at the edge of a cliff.

They broke into the base. They captured Captain Phasma, a First Order stormtrooper, and made her shut down the shields. Then they found Rey! Chewie howled when he saw her. They were all together again.

But the Resistance needed more help. Their attack wasn't going as planned. First Order ships were overwhelming the Resistance fighters.

Han and Chewbacca broke into Starkiller Base's oscillator and planted explosives. But before they could leave, Han had to stop Kylo Ren. Kylo was his son but had turned to the dark side of the Force. Chewbacca watched as Han tried to talk to his son. But the dark side was too powerful—and Kylo slayed his father.

Chewbacca howled in sadness. 🐻 He fired on Kylo Ren and injured him. Then, Chewbacca detonated all of the explosives. The oscillator was blowing up! Chewbacca, Finn, and Rey raced out of the base.

When Chewbacca returned to the *Millennium Falcon*,
he found Rey in the snow. She and Finn had been fighting
Kylo Ren. Finn was hurt! Chewbacca roared  as he
carried Finn on board. They escaped Starkiller Base just
as it was about to explode. The Resistance had won!

At the Resistance base, Chewbacca readied the
Millennium Falcon. He and Rey were going to use the map
to find Luke Skywalker! Chewie howled a goodbye to
his Resistance friends as the *Millennium Falcon* took
off on a new adventure.